The Legacy of Project Akashdeep

Mrigendra Bharti

Published by Sellbrochure Vymish Entertainment, 2024.

This is a work of fiction. Similarities to real people, places, or events are entirely coincidental.

THE LEGACY OF PROJECT AKASHDEEP

First edition. July 5, 2024.

ISBN: 979-8227300683

Written by Mrigendra Bharti.

Table of Contents

A Preface: The Legacy of Project Akashdeep

Across the vast expanse of space, a faint whisper once stirred – a signal from a distant world, a tentative bridge reaching out from the unknown. It was a flicker of hope in a universe teeming with silence, a spark that ignited a fire of curiosity within humanity. This book is the story of that fire, the chronicle of a project that dared to dream beyond the boundaries of our planet – Project Akashdeep.

This is not just a tale of scientific breakthroughs and technological marvels. It's a testament to the enduring power of human collaboration, a story where artists and scientists, dreamers and pragmatists, joined hands to bridge the gap between two worlds. It's a saga of courage, where a small crew ventured into the unknown, facing the wonders and perils of the cosmos to secure a future not just for Earth, but for a newfound civilization.

Within these pages, you will encounter Maya, a seasoned commander driven by a thirst for exploration. You'll meet Lyra, her Akashdeep counterpart, whose calm demeanor masks a steely resolve. Amara, the brilliant scientist with a passion for sustainable solutions, and Elara, the visionary astrophysicist who dared to dream of interstellar travel, will guide you through their groundbreaking discoveries. And alongside them, Kai and Kiran, the artists who translated the wonders of the universe into breathtaking expressions, reminding us that even in the face of scientific exploration, the human spirit craves beauty.

The Legacy of Project Akashdeep is a story of challenges overcome, lessons learned, and a future forged through unity. It's a reminder that while the universe may be vast and our place within it seemingly insignificant, the human spirit, when fueled by collaboration and a shared vision, can reach for the stars and illuminate the path forward.

Prepare to embark on a journey beyond the boundaries of our world, a testament to the enduring legacy of Project Akashdeep.

A Prologue: The Legacy of Project Akashdeep

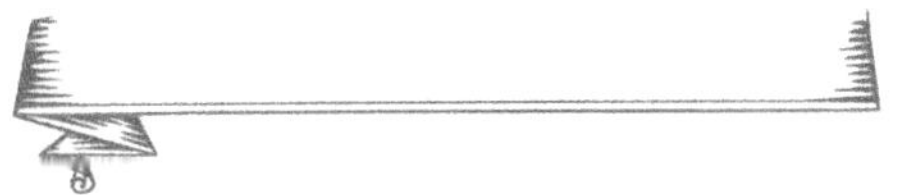

The year is 2042. Earth, once a vibrant tapestry of nations, has become a unified force, its gaze turned to the stars. Decades of environmental crises had forged a new global consciousness, pushing humanity to seek a sustainable future. It was during this period of introspection that the faintest of signals, a whisper across the cosmic void, pierced the silence.

The origin: Akashdeep, a world long shrouded in myth and legend. The signal, a complex series of electromagnetic pulses, held a captivating message – a plea for assistance, a beacon of hope from a civilization teetering on the brink.

Project Akashdeep was born from this cosmic whisper. A collaborative effort unlike any other, it brought together the brightest minds from Earth – scientists, engineers, and artists. The mission was audacious – to travel across the vast gulf of space, establish communication, and understand the plight of the Akashdeep people.

This prologue takes us back further, to the very birthplace of the project. We find ourselves in a bustling research facility, its walls adorned with astronomical charts and holographic projections of celestial bodies. Dr. Anya Sharma, a renowned astrophysicist with eyes that mirrored the vastness of space, stands before a team of eager scientists and engineers.

"The signal," she begins, her voice filled with awe and a hint of trepidation, "is unlike anything we've ever encountered. It carries a wealth of information, a language we're slowly deciphering. But one thing is clear – Akashdeep is in dire need of our help."

The room buzzes with excitement and nervous energy. A young engineer, his face a canvas of ambition, raises his hand. "Is interstellar travel even a possibility?"

Anya smiles, a glint of determination in her eyes. "There's much we don't know, but that's the beauty of this project. We are pioneers, pushing the boundaries of what's possible. Together, we will build a bridge across the stars, a bridge that will not only connect us to Akashdeep, but usher in a new era of human exploration."

This is the story of that bridge, a testament to human ingenuity and collaboration. It's a story whispered on the wind, carried across the cosmos, waiting to be heard.

About Sellbrochure Vymish Entertainment

Sellbrochure Vymish Entertainment, recognized as India's largest book publishing company, has made significant strides in ensuring its extensive collection of books reaches audiences across the global market. This rapid expansion is a testament to the company's dedication to disseminating knowledge and literature far beyond national borders. Central to its success is its affiliation with InkWhirl Media Networks, a reputable entity in the media and publication industry known for its innovative and strategic approaches. Within this network, InkWhirl Publication LLC operates as a vital division, further enhancing the company's capabilities and reach in the international market.

The visionary behind this enterprise is Mrigendra Bharti, the founder of Sellbrochure Vymish Entertainment. His foresight and passion for the literary world have been instrumental in steering the company towards remarkable growth and recognition. Under his leadership, Sellbrochure Vymish Entertainment has not only expanded its catalog but also established a strong presence in both domestic and international markets. Mrigendra Bharti's commitment to excellence and innovation has been a driving force in the company's journey, ensuring that it stays ahead of industry trends and meets the evolving needs of readers worldwide.

Sellbrochure Vymish Entertainment operates under the robust support of its parental organization, Mrigendra Bharti Group InfoTech. This affiliation provides the necessary resources and strategic guidance, enabling the publishing company to undertake ambitious projects and explore new markets. Mrigendra Bharti Group InfoTech's extensive experience in technology and information services has been a valuable asset, allowing Sellbrochure Vymish Entertainment to integrate advanced digital solutions in its operations, thereby enhancing its distribution capabilities and reader engagement.

Through relentless efforts and a commitment to quality, Sellbrochure Vymish Entertainment continues to break barriers and expand the reach of Indian literature globally. The company's diverse portfolio includes a wide range of genres, catering to different age groups and interests, thereby fostering a rich and inclusive reading culture. As it continues to innovate and grow, Sellbrochure Vymish Entertainment remains dedicated to its mission of making literature accessible to all, contributing significantly to the global literary landscape.

Connect With Mrigendra,

Thank you very much for choosing this book.

You can also connect with me on Instagram,

https://www.instagram.com/i_mrigendrabharti.official

With Love,

Mrigendra Bharti

Introduction

Humanity, once a species consumed by internal conflict, had finally turned its gaze to the stars. The scars of environmental negligence served as a stark reminder of their past, yet fueled a fervent desire for a sustainable future. It was during this period of introspection that a faint whisper, a cosmic anomaly, pierced the silence.

This wasn't mere radio static; it was a complex message, a beacon of hope emanating from a distant world – Akashdeep. Long shrouded in myth and legend, Akashdeep's plea for assistance resonated across the globe. The message, a desperate plea for help amidst an undisclosed crisis, ignited a spark of unity within humanity.

Project Akashdeep, a collaborative effort unlike any other, was born from this interstellar whisper. It wasn't just about scientific advancement; it was a bridge of empathy, a testament to humanity's newfound ability to look beyond its own borders and extend a helping hand.

This isn't just a chronicle of technological marvels and groundbreaking discoveries. It's a story woven from the threads of human connection – the unwavering courage of Maya, the Earth commander driven by a thirst for exploration; the calm resolve of Lyra, her Akashdeep counterpart; the brilliant scientific minds of Amara and Elara, one driven by sustainable solutions, the other by the dream of interstellar travel; and the artistic souls of Kai and Kiran, who translated the wonders of the cosmos into breathtaking expressions.

"The Legacy of Project Akashdeep" is a testament to the enduring power of collaboration. It's a testament to the human spirit that, when fueled by a shared vision, can reach for the stars and illuminate a path forward. It's a story of challenges overcome, lessons learned, and a future forged through unity. It's a reminder that while the universe may be vast and our place within it seemingly insignificant, even the faintest whisper can ignite a fire of hope, a fire that can bridge the gap between worlds and illuminate a path towards a brighter future.

Prepare to embark on a journey beyond the boundaries of our world, a testament to the enduring legacy of Project Akashdeep.

Chapter 1: The Hidden Message

The year is 2047. Neo-Delhi, once a bustling metropolis, now resembled a dystopian nightmare choked by a perpetual haze. The relentless sun, filtered through layers of smog, cast an orange glow over the city, turning even the most vibrant colors into a muted palette of rust and ochre. Towering chrome and glass buildings, once symbols of progress, were now silhouettes shrouded in a thick, acrid fog.

Seventeen-year-old Maya, her face smudged with grease and sweat, squinted through the haze as she navigated the labyrinthine alleys of Chandni Chowk, the old city center. Her nimble fingers expertly dismantled a rusted engine block, salvaging any usable parts. The air hung heavy with the metallic tang of exhaust fumes and the acrid bite of burning plastic. It was a familiar smell, a constant companion in this concrete jungle.

Maya wasn't born in this smog-choked world. Grainy vids her grandmother cherished spoke of a time when the sky was blue, and lush green parks replaced these towering monstrosities. Those were relics of a bygone era, a time before the Great Ecological Collapse. Now, survival was a daily struggle. Every spare part Maya salvaged, every scrap of metal she could barter for, meant another meal for her ailing grandmother and a few credits closer to their dream – a filtration unit for their cramped apartment, a sliver of clean air in this suffocating city.

The oppressive heat bounced off the cracked pavement, shimmering like a mirage. Maya wiped her brow with the back of her grease-stained hand, her dark eyes scanning the overflowing bins and discarded machinery for hidden treasures. Her worn canvas satchel bulged with retrieved components – a dented gear, a length of frayed wire, a chipped circuit board. Each held the potential for a second life, a chance to be repurposed into something useful.

Suddenly, a guttural cough erupted from a nearby alley. Maya, ever cautious, grabbed the rusty wrench she used for self-defense and approached with wary steps. Huddled in the shadows was an old man, his frail frame wracked with hacking coughs. His clothes were a patchwork of faded fabric, and his hands trembled as he clutched a battered suitcase.

"Are you alright, baba?" Maya asked, her voice a mixture of concern and practiced street smarts.

The old man wheezed, his voice raspy from disuse. "Just... need some air," he rasped, gesturing weakly at the clogged sky.

Hesitantly, Maya lowered her wrench. Something about the man's desperation resonated with her. She rummaged in her bag and pulled out a small, crumpled water filter she always carried. It wouldn't provide much, but it was something.

The man took the filter with trembling hands and offered a grateful smile. "Thank you, bachchi. You have a kind heart in a harsh world."

"Just trying to survive, baba," Maya replied, a hint of bitterness in her voice.

The old man's gaze lingered on her satchel. "You're a tinkerer, aren't you?"

Maya shrugged, her defenses rising again. Knowledge was power in these parts, especially knowledge of how to fix things.

"I have something for you," the old man said, his voice gaining strength. He fumbled with his suitcase, his gnarled fingers finally producing a small, tarnished metal box.

Maya eyed the box with suspicion. It was beautifully crafted, etched with intricate patterns that seemed vaguely familiar. Her grandmother told stories of ancient India, a time of skilled artisans and forgotten knowledge. Could this box hold a relic from that lost era?

"What is it?" she asked, her voice a wary whisper.

The old man smiled, a spark of mischief lighting up his rheumy eyes. "A gift," he said, his voice raspy but firm. "Something that might change your luck, bachchi."

As Maya hesitantly accepted the box, it felt unexpectedly cool against her calloused palm. Curiosity warred with caution. She knew better than to trust strangers, especially in this unforgiving city. However, the desperation in the old man's eyes and the promise of something more than just another scrap of metal gnawed at her.

With a curt nod, Maya thanked the old man, her gaze lingering on his retreating figure. He shuffled away, disappearing deeper into the maze of alleys like a wisp of smoke.

Back in her cramped apartment, Maya examined the box. It was surprisingly light, made from a metal that seemed to shimmer with an otherworldly sheen. She traced the intricate patterns with her fingers, the strange symbols sending a shiver down her spine.

Her grandmother, frail and coughing in the corner, watched with a curious glint in her eyes. "What have you got there, Maya?" she rasped.

"An old man gave it to me," Maya replied, setting the box down on the rickety table. She pried it open with a screwdriver, revealing a contraption unlike anything she'd ever seen.

It wasn't a weapon or a tool, that much was clear. It resembled a radio, but it had dials and knobs unlike any modern technology. The central panel was filled with glowing green tubes, pulsating with an ethereal light.

"Looks like something from your grandmother's stories," Maya said with a grin, nudging the old woman playfully.

A flicker of recognition crossed her grandmother's eyes. "The Akashvani," she whispered, her voice barely a croak.

"Akashvani?" Maya echoed, the name sounding strangely familiar. Had she heard it in one of her grandmother's stories?

"The voice of the sky," her grandmother explained, her voice gaining strength with each word. "Whispers from the forgotten times, stories of a world beyond the stars."

Maya's skepticism warred with a thrilling spark of curiosity. Could this be more than just an old relic? Could it be a connection to something bigger, something beyond the smog-choked reality of Neo-Delhi?

She gingerly picked up the device, her fingers brushing against the strange metal. A tingling sensation ran through her arm, almost electrical in nature. Intrigued, she fiddled with the knobs, her brow furrowed in concentration.

Decades of tinkering with discarded electronics had given Maya an intuitive understanding of machinery. She carefully adjusted the dials, following an instinct she couldn't explain. Slowly, a coarse hiss filled the room, followed by a crackle of static. Maya leaned closer, her breath catching in her throat.

From the static, a faint whisper emerged, a distorted voice speaking in an unknown language. It was melodic and haunting, filled with an otherworldly cadence. The glowing green tubes pulsed faster, the device emanating a faint hum.

Despite not understanding the words, Maya felt a strange sense of connection, a pull towards something unseen. This wasn't just static; it was a message, a voice yearning to be heard. As the hours passed, Maya became engrossed, spending the night meticulously adjusting the dials, trying to decipher the message.

The next morning, the apartment was bathed in the harsh orange light of the smog-filled sky. Maya, exhausted but wired, studied the device. The voice had faded, the static replaced by an eerie silence. Had she imagined it all? The doubts gnawed at her.

Her grandmother, however, seemed invigorated. A youthful spark shone in her eyes, a testament to the forgotten stories awakened by the Akashvani. She urged Maya to continue, to unravel the message, to find the source of the voice.

Fueled by her grandmother's newfound enthusiasm and her own nagging curiosity, Maya dove deep into research. She scoured through dusty libraries and the vast digital archives of the Neo-Delhi network. The Akashvani wasn't a mere relic.

It was mentioned in ancient texts, shrouded in myth and legend.

The stories varied, some claiming it was a device used by ancient scientists to communicate with celestial beings. Others spoke of a gateway, a portal to another dimension – a paradise untouched by pollution and the ravages of time. This resonated deeply with Maya. A world beyond the choking smog, a place of clean air and vibrant life – it seemed like a desperate dream, a figment of forgotten folklore.

But the faint glimmer of hope ignited a fire within her. The cryptic message from the Akashvani, the longing in the voice, it all pointed towards something real, something beyond the despair of Neo-Delhi. Maya spent hours deciphering the symbols on the device, comparing them to ancient scripts found in dusty archives. Her days blurred into nights, fueled by adrenaline and a growing sense of purpose.

One evening, as she hunched over a flickering microfiche reader, a pattern emerged. The symbols on the Akashvani matched a fragment from an ancient text, a reference to a hidden location in the Himalayas. The coordinates were vague, cryptic references to celestial bodies and geographical landmarks long lost to time.

A surge of excitement coursed through Maya. The message wasn't just a whisper from the past. It was a coded map, a key to unlocking something extraordinary. Sharing a glance with her grandmother, Maya knew she couldn't ignore this call. This wasn't just about a mythical paradise; it was about hope, about finding a better future for them both.

The journey, however, would be fraught with danger. The Himalayas were a treacherous landscape, guarded by harsh weather and elusive creatures. More importantly, if the legends were true, the Akashvani was a powerful device. Powerful enough to attract the wrong kind of attention.

But Maya wasn't one to back down from a challenge. With a newfound determination glinting in her eyes, she began to make preparations. She scoured online forums, seeking information on the Himalayas, on survival tactics, and on scavenging for supplies in a world where every scrap had value.

She knew she couldn't embark on this journey alone. There was Rohan, her best friend, a tech prodigy with an uncanny talent for unlocking digital secrets. And there was Rishi, a gruff ex-military man who lived in the apartment below them, a solitary figure shrouded in mystery. Their skills, combined with Maya's resourcefulness, might give them a fighting chance in the unforgiving wilderness.

As Maya gazed at the Akashvani, glowing faintly on the table, the voice from the cosmos seemed to whisper again, a call to adventure that resonated deep within her soul. This was more than just a relic; it was a chance to escape the suffocating reality of Neo-Delhi, a chance to find the fabled Akashdeep and a glimpse of a brighter tomorrow.

The decision hung heavy in the air. Sharing the secret of the Akashvani and the potential existence of Akashdeep, the fabled gateway, was a gamble. Maya knew the dangers involved – the harsh terrain of the Himalayas, the possibility of hostile forces guarding the entrance, and the sheer improbability of the legend itself.

Yet, the longing in her grandmother's eyes and the flickering hope within her own heart were undeniable. This wasn't just about a mythical paradise; it was about a chance, a possibility of a better life beyond the smog-choked reality of Neo-Delhi.

First, Maya sought out Rohan, her tech-savvy partner in crime. He was hunched over his workstation, a tangled mess of wires and discarded circuits surrounding him. He looked up, his dark eyes gleaming with curiosity when Maya entered.

"Got something to show you," Maya announced, placing the Akashvani on the table with a dramatic flourish.

Rohan's skepticism was evident. He scrutinized the device, his fingers tracing the strange symbols. "A relic you say? Doesn't look very reliable."

Maya recounted her experience, the faint whisper she heard, the coded message, and the coordinates pointing towards the Himalayas. Rohan listened intently, his skepticism gradually morphing into intrigue. As Maya detailed the stories of Akashdeep, a flicker of excitement sparked in his eyes.

"A gateway to another dimension, huh?" Rohan mused, tapping his chin. "Sounds like something straight out of the old vid games."

"Maybe," Maya conceded, "but the coordinates... they seem real. And the message, Rohan, it felt real too."

With his usual eagerness, Rohan dove into deciphering the coordinates. He cross-referenced them with ancient maps and satellite imagery, his fingers flying across the keyboard. After a tense hour of digital exploration, he slammed his fist on the desk with a triumphant grin.

"Found it!" he exclaimed. "A remote location deep within the Himalayas. Matches the celestial references perfectly."

A wave of exhilaration washed over Maya. The coordinates were real, the legend of Akashdeep might actually hold some truth. But before they could celebrate, another concern surfaced.

"We can't exactly stroll into the Himalayas and ask for directions to a magical gateway," Maya pointed out.

"True," Rohan agreed, stroking his chin thoughtfully. "We'll need a guide, someone familiar with the mountains, someone who can get us there in one piece."

Their solution lived right below their apartment – Rishi, the ex-military man with a haunted past and an air of mystery that clung to him like a shroud. He rarely interacted with them, but his gruff demeanor often masked a quiet observance.

Taking a deep breath, Maya descended the rickety staircase, the worn metal echoing with her determined steps. She knocked on Rishi's door, the sound echoing through the silent hallway. After a long pause, the door creaked open, revealing Rishi's weathered face.

"Maya?" he asked, a hint of surprise in his voice. "What can I do for you?"

Taking a deep breath, Maya plunged into the story, explaining the Akashvani, the message, and the coordinates pointing towards Akashdeep. She held her breath as Rishi listened intently, his expression unreadable.

Finally, after a long pause, he spoke. "Akashdeep," he muttered, the name rolling off his tongue with a hint of familiarity. "That's a story I haven't heard in a long time."

Hope surged through Maya. Did Rishi know something about the fabled gateway? Could he be the guide they desperately needed?

"You know something about it?" Rohan pressed, leaning forward in anticipation.

Rishi's gaze flickered towards the Akashvani, his eyes filled with a complex mix of emotions. "I might," he said finally, "and whether you believe it or not, I might be the only one who can get you there. But this journey will be fraught with danger. Are you sure you're all prepared for what you might find?"

Maya exchanged a determined glance with Rohan. The allure of hope, the desperate yearning for a better future, outweighed the fear of the unknown. With a resolute nod, Maya spoke for both of them.

"We're ready."

Chapter 2: Into the Himalayas

The air crackled with a nervous energy as Maya, Rohan, and Rishi stood at the edge of Neo-Delhi, the smog-shrouded city sprawling behind them like a decaying monument to a bygone era. Their backpacks bulged with salvaged supplies – scavenged climbing gear, water purification tablets, and solar panels to charge Rohan's essential gadgets. The crisp mountain air, though tinged with the faintest whisper of exhaust fumes carried by the wind, felt like a luxury compared to the ever-present haze of Neo-Delhi.

Rishi, a stark contrast to his youthful companions, exuded an aura of quiet competence. His worn, weather-beaten face held the secrets of countless expeditions, and his eyes, steely grey under a well-worn baseball cap, held a depth of experience that spoke of past dangers.

Their journey began with a rickety local bus, packed with weathered faces and curious stares. They disembarked at a dusty village nestled at the foothills of the Himalayas, the towering peaks scraping the clear blue sky. Here, the air vibrated with the melodic calls of unseen birds and the rustling of wind through ancient trees.

Finding a local guide proved more difficult than expected. The villagers, though welcoming, eyed the trio with suspicion. The legend of Akashdeep was whispered in hushed tones, a myth shrouded in fear and superstition. Finally, an old woman with eyes like pools of molten gold stepped forward, her wrinkled face etched with a map of past experiences.

"Akashdeep," she rasped, her voice like dry leaves rustling in the wind. "A place of power, guarded by spirits and watched by watchful eyes. You seek it for good reasons, I can feel it in your bones. But be warned, child, the path is fraught with peril. Are you ready?"

Maya, her heart pounding with a mix of excitement and apprehension, spoke for them all. "We are ready, Nani. We have no choice."

The old woman nodded solemnly. She revealed a weathered map, its edges frayed and symbols faded. It depicted a treacherous route, marked with cryptic warnings and ancient landmarks. She explained the path, her voice filled with a reverence bordering on fear.

Thus began their ascent. The initial enthusiasm quickly gave way to grueling reality. The path, a narrow trail winding through dense forests, tested their stamina. The thin mountain air made breathing a conscious effort, and the steep inclines challenged their endurance. Days blurred into nights, filled with the rhythmic sound of their own footsteps and the constant murmur of unseen streams.

Rohan, despite his initial complaints about leaving behind his beloved gadgets, proved surprisingly adept. His nimble fingers, once used for intricate circuit repairs, found surprising dexterity in setting up camp and identifying edible plants. Maya, fueled by a relentless determination, led the way, her knowledge of scavenging proving invaluable in finding shelter and fixing broken equipment.

Rishi, however, remained an enigma. He moved with the silent grace of a predator, his weathered face betraying no emotion. He spoke only when necessary, his words filled with a stoic pragmatism. Yet, there were moments when Maya would catch him gazing at the snow-capped peaks, a flicker of something akin to longing in his eyes.

One evening, as they huddled around a crackling campfire, Maya finally broke the silence. "Rishi, why are you helping us? You know the risks involved."

Rishi stirred the fire embers with a long stick. "Akashdeep," he finally muttered, "holds secrets, child. Secrets that reach far beyond mere legends."

He hesitated, then continued, his voice a low murmur. "I once... sought it myself. For reasons I cannot speak of now. But the journey changed me. Perhaps, by helping you, I can find some measure of redemption."

His words hung heavy in the air, sparking a surge of unspoken questions in Maya's mind. What secrets did Rishi hold? What was his past connection to Akashdeep? But before she could press further, a loud howl pierced the silence, echoing through the valley like a mournful cry.

The howl ripped through the stillness of the night, a chilling sound that sent shivers down Maya's spine. Rohan flinched, his gaze darting nervously towards the dark forest surrounding them. Rishi, however, sprang to his feet, a predator suddenly alert.

"Stay close," he commanded, his voice low and urgent. He grabbed a worn leather rucksack from beside him and pulled out what looked like a makeshift hunting rifle, its barrel cobbled together from scavenged parts.

Adrenaline surged through Maya's veins. The stories of the mountain whispered of yeti, mythical beasts that haunted the high altitudes. Could that be what they were facing?

As if responding to her unspoken fear, Rishi spoke again. "Not yeti," he muttered, his eyes scanning the darkness. "Something else."

Crouching low, they followed Rishi deeper into the woods, the flickering campfire light fading behind them. The forest floor was a labyrinth of roots and fallen branches, the darkness thick enough to taste. The wind whistled through the trees, carrying the chilling howls at irregular intervals.

Suddenly, a flicker of movement in the undergrowth caught Maya's eye. A pair of glowing yellow eyes emerged from the darkness, followed by a low growl that sent a jolt of fear through her. It wasn't the monstrous yeti of legend, but a creature far more familiar and dangerous – a pack of wild dogs, their eyes reflecting the dying embers of their campfire.

Rohan, ever resourceful, fumbled with his backpack. "Found it!" he exclaimed, pulling out a modified flashlight with a flickering strobe light. With a defiant yell, he aimed the light at the approaching pack.

The dogs, startled by the sudden burst of light, hesitated. The strobe effect, flickering erratically, seemed to confuse them. Taking advantage of the momentary disorientation, Rishi let out a loud, primal roar, charging forward with his makeshift rifle raised. The unexpected assault further startled the wild dogs, and they yelped, scattering back into the darkness.

Breathing heavily, they regrouped by the dying embers of the campfire. Rohan, his face pale, collapsed onto a log. "That was close," he muttered, wiping sweat from his brow.

Rishi remained vigilant, his gaze fixed on the dark woods. "Not over yet," he said, his voice grim. "Wild dogs travel in packs. They'll be back."

The night stretched on, filled with the tense anticipation of another attack. They took turns resting, their sleep fragmented and haunted by the chilling howls. But the dogs didn't return. By morning, an eerie silence had settled over the forest.

As they continued their trek, the encounter with the wild dogs cast a shadow of uncertainty over their journey. The mountains, once majestic and inspiring, now seemed to hold an unseen threat. Maya couldn't shake the feeling of being watched, of unseen eyes following them through the dense foliage.

Days turned into weeks. The landscape changed dramatically, the lush greenery giving way to a stark, rocky terrain. The air grew colder, the bite of wind sharper. They encountered snow patches, remnants of winter clinging stubbornly to the high slopes.

The path became increasingly treacherous, a narrow ribbon of rock clinging precariously to the mountainside. One wrong step could mean a fatal fall. Rishi's knowledge of the mountain terrain proved invaluable, his surefootedness guiding them through treacherous slopes and across rickety rope bridges spanning yawning chasms.

One evening, as they huddled around a meager campfire, Rohan pointed towards the horizon. Towering above them, against the backdrop of a fiery sunset, stood a massive, snow-capped peak unlike any they had seen before. A sense of awe washed over them. This was it. This was where the map led them.

"Akashdeep," Rishi whispered, his voice filled with a mixture of dread and reverence. They stood at the threshold of legend, the gateway to a mythical reality. But the journey was far from over. The true test, it seemed, lay just beyond the snow-capped peak, shrouded in mist and guarded by secrets of the past.

The ascent to the peak of Akashdeep was a grueling challenge. The air grew thin, each breath a struggle. Snow crunched under their boots, and the wind whipped their faces with icy needles. Rishi, however, seemed unfazed. He led the way with practiced ease, navigating treacherous slopes with the agility of a mountain goat.

As they neared the summit, the landscape changed dramatically. The stark rock face gave way to a series of ancient stone structures, half-buried in snow. Their weathered surfaces bore intricate carvings, symbols that echoed the patterns etched on the Akashvani device. A sense of awe and wonder crept over Maya. This wasn't just a mountain; it was a forgotten city, a place built by a civilization long lost to time.

Reaching the summit, they found themselves standing on a plateau shrouded in a swirling mist. In the distance, a colossal structure emerged from the swirling clouds, resembling a giant monolith reaching towards the sky. It was made from the same black, metallic material as the Akashvani, glowing with a faint, ethereal light.

As they approached cautiously, the faint sounds of chanting reached their ears. A low, rhythmic hum resonated in the air, pulsating through the very ground beneath their feet. Curiosity warred with trepidation. Who or what inhabited this place? Were they friends or foes?

Rishi raised a hand, signaling for them to stop. He knelt down and examined the ground, a furrow appearing on his brow. He traced an intricate symbol etched on a flat stone with his finger. "The language of the ancients," he muttered, his voice filled with a newfound urgency.

Suddenly, a figure emerged from the swirling mist. It was a tall, slender humanoid figure, cloaked in shimmering white robes. Its face was obscured by a hood, but its eyes glowed with an ethereal blue light.

Rohan and Maya exchanged nervous glances. This wasn't what they expected. Rishi, however, seemed to recognize the figure. He spoke in a language that sounded melodic yet unfamiliar to Maya's ears.

The figure responded in the same tongue, its voice echoing with an otherworldly resonance. The conversation continued, a tense exchange filled with unspoken questions and cryptic answers.

Finally, Rishi turned to face them. "They are the guardians," he explained, his voice tight with contained emotion. "They have been waiting for the one who can speak the language of the Akashvani."

He gestured towards Maya, a flicker of hope gleaming in his eyes. "They believe you are that one." Suddenly, the weight of responsibility settled on Maya's shoulders. She, a scavenger girl from the smog-choked streets of Neo-Delhi, held the key to unlocking the secrets of Akashdeep? Her heart pounded, a mixture of fear and determination coursing through her veins. Stepping forward, she grasped the cool metal of the Akashvani, feeling a strange energy pulse through her fingers. She looked at the figure, its glowing eyes seemingly peering into her soul.

Taking a deep breath, Maya began to speak. The words flowed through her, a language she somehow understood, a message carried on the faint whispers from the Akashvani. The air crackled with an electric energy as the message unfolded, a plea for help, a longing for a connection with a world beyond the stars.

As her words resonated across the vast expanse of the mountain peak, the shimmering monolith pulsed with a blinding light. The swirling mist parted, revealing a breathtaking vista – a lush, vibrant world bathed in the golden light of a distant sun. This was Akashdeep, a haven untouched by the pollution and decay of Earth, a glimpse of a future they had only dared to dream of.

The revelation before them was like a punch to the gut. Akashdeep, a paradise suspended in the sky, shimmered with an unimaginable beauty. Lush green forests stretched into the distance, dotted with glistening crystal-clear lakes reflecting the golden light of a second sun. It defied everything Maya knew, everything she thought possible.

The guardian, its robed figure still shrouded in mystery, seemed to observe their reactions with an impassive gaze. Maya, her brain reeling, found herself stepping forward, drawn by an irresistible pull towards the gateway. But a hand clamped on her shoulder, stopping her in her tracks.

Rishi stood beside her, his face etched with a complex mix of emotions. "Wait, Maya," he said, his voice low and urgent. "Think about what this means. Leaving Earth might seem like a dream come true, but what about your grandmother? What about Rohan?"

His words struck a chord in Maya's heart. The initial euphoria gave way to a wave of doubt. Could she truly abandon everything she knew, everything she cared about, for this paradise? What about the message she received, the plea for help? Was it all a trap?

Rohan, who had been staring in speechless awe at Akashdeep, finally spoke. "Maybe," he said, his voice tinged with uncertainty, "we can figure out a way to bridge the worlds. Share the knowledge of Akashdeep with Earth, find a way to heal the planet."

His suggestion ignited a spark of hope within Maya. Perhaps there was another way. Perhaps they weren't destined for an all-or-nothing choice. She turned towards the guardian, a question forming on her lips.

"Is there... a way for us to return?" she asked, her voice trembling slightly.

The guardian tilted its head, a gesture that somehow conveyed understanding. A wave of energy emanated from its outstretched hand, flowing into the Akashvani device. The symbols on its surface glowed with renewed intensity.

Suddenly, Maya understood. The Akashvani wasn't just a receiver; it was a key, a two-way bridge. It could not only bridge the gap between dimensions but also create a connection, a means of communication.

Looking at Rohan and Rishi, Maya felt a surge of determination. They had stumbled upon something far greater than a mere escape route. They had the potential to create a future where Earth and Akashdeep could co-exist, where knowledge and resources could be shared.

Turning back towards the shimmering gateway, Maya held the Akashvani aloft. "Take us back," she declared, her voice ringing with newfound purpose. "But not just us. Let this be a message, a bridge between worlds. Let us learn from each other and heal our planet together."

The guardian's form shimmered, its blue eyes seeming to hold a flicker of approval. With a blinding flash of light, the world around them dissolved. When their vision cleared, they found themselves back on the snow-covered peak, the swirling mist once again obscuring the gateway to Akashdeep.

Akashdeep was no longer a fleeting glimpse but a tangible reality. The journey had just begun, a journey that held the promise of a better tomorrow, not just for them, but for the entire world.

As they descended the treacherous slopes of the Himalayas, Maya knew their mission had changed. They were no longer just scavengers or a tech-savvy boy. They were ambassadors, tasked with carrying a message of hope and forging a future where the skies of Earth could shine as brightly as the golden sun of Akashdeep.

Chapter 3: Whispers Across Worlds

The descent from Akashdeep was fraught with its own challenges. Exhaustion gnawed at their limbs, their bodies still reeling from the physical and emotional upheaval they experienced. Yet, a newfound purpose fueled their steps. They weren't merely returning home; they were carrying a message, a bridge woven between worlds.

Back in the dusty village nestled at the foothills, their arrival was met with astonishment. The villagers, used to seeing weary travelers descend from the mountains, found something different in their eyes – a spark of hope, a newfound resolve.

News of their encounter with the guardians of Akashdeep spread like wildfire. The legend, long whispered in hushed tones, took on a new reality. Villagers approached them, their faces etched with curiosity and a desperate yearning for a better future.

Maya found herself in the role of an unlikely leader. Using the knowledge gleaned from the Akashvani and her own experiences, she began to explain the concept of Akashdeep, a world beyond their polluted skies, a place of clean air and vibrant life. Her words ignited a flicker of hope in their eyes.

Rohan, ever the tech whiz, delved into the mechanics of the Akashvani. He spent days meticulously studying the device, deciphering its complex functions. His goal? To establish a permanent link between Earth and Akashdeep, a channel for communication, a bridge for sharing knowledge.

Rishi, however, remained on the periphery. His silence spoke volumes. His haunted past, his connection to

Akashdeep, remained a mystery. Maya knew there was more to his story, secrets he wasn't yet ready to share.

One evening, as they huddled around a crackling fire, an elder from the village approached them. He was a wizened man, his face etched with the wisdom of years spent weathering the harsh Himalayan climate.

"The guardians spoke of a plea," he said, his voice raspy but firm. "A cry for help. Can you tell us more?"

Maya nodded, a heavy responsibility settling on her shoulders. She relayed the message she received, the desperate longing for a connection with a world beyond the stars. The villagers listened intently, their faces etched with a mixture of wonder and concern.

"They need something from us," a young woman spoke up, her voice trembling slightly. "But what? What can we offer a world untouched by our pollution?"

The question hung heavy in the air. Akashdeep, a paradise, seemed to have everything they lacked. What value could a world choked by smog and ravaged by greed possibly offer?

A flicker of an idea sparked in Maya's mind. The answer, she realized, wasn't about materialistic things. It was about something intangible, something they held in abundance – their resilience, their spirit of innovation, and their ability to adapt even in the face of adversity.

"Perhaps," Maya began, her voice gaining strength, "they don't need our resources. Perhaps they need what we've learned from our mistakes. Our ingenuity in forging a life even in a harsh environment. Maybe they can learn from our struggles and avoid repeating them."

Her words resonated with the villagers. They spent the next few days sharing their stories, showcasing their resourcefulness in repurposing scavenged materials, their techniques for growing crops in limited spaces. Their struggles, it seemed, held a value they hadn't considered before.

As days turned into weeks, a collaboration began to blossom. The villagers, under Maya's guidance, started documenting their knowledge in a universal language embedded within the Akashvani. Rohan, with tireless dedication, toiled away on the device, pushing its limits to establish a stable connection.

And Rishi? He remained a silent observer, occasionally offering glimpses of his expertise in deciphering advanced features of the Akashdeep technology. One evening, as they huddled around the fire, he finally addressed Maya directly.

"You're doing well, Maya," he said, a touch of pride in his voice. "You've united them, given them a purpose. You remind me..." His voice trailed off, a flicker of sadness crossing his face.

"Remind you of what?" Maya pressed, curiosity piqued. A long silence followed before Rishi finally spoke, his voice barely a whisper. "Of what Akashdeep once was, and what it may become again."

His words sparked a question that had been simmering within Maya for weeks. It was time to confront the secrets Rishi held so close. "Tell me, Rishi," she began, her voice filled with resolve, "what is your connection to Akashdeep?"

Rishi's shoulders slumped, the firelight casting long shadows across his weathered face. For a long moment, he stared into the flickering flames, a battle raging within him. Finally, with a sigh, he spoke.

"It was a different time," he began, his voice low and raspy. "The world wasn't always choked by smog. The skies were clear, and the stars shone brightly. I was young then, a soldier fighting in a war fueled by greed and shortsightedness."

He paused, his eyes filled with a haunting sadness. "The war ravaged the planet. We used technology far beyond what you can imagine, weapons of unimaginable power. The consequences were swift and devastating."

Rishi's voice cracked with emotion. "The air became choked with pollution, the land barren and lifeless. Civilization as we knew it crumbled. Only a few of us survived, scattered pockets of humanity clinging to existence in a world of our own making."

A spark of realization dawned on Maya. Rishi wasn't just a seasoned explorer; he was a survivor, a witness to the very devastation that threatened their own world. "Akashdeep," she whispered, "was it a refuge?"

Rishi nodded grimly. "A project initiated before the war, a place where humanity could start over, a world untouched by our mistakes." He gestured towards the Akashvani device resting on the table. "This device was the key, a bridge that allowed communication and resource exchange."

He explained how the connection between worlds eventually faltered, the technology failing under the weight of the deteriorating environment. Akashdeep, he believed, remained unaware of the fate that befell their home planet.

"Then why the plea?" Rohan chimed in, his brow furrowed in thought. "If they don't know—"

"They may have felt the tremors," Rishi interrupted. "The disruption in the connection. A faint echo of our suffering, a warning of what might be their future."

A heavy silence descended upon them. The weight of history pressed down on them, the past a stark reminder of the consequences of unchecked greed. But amidst the despair, a flicker of hope remained.

"Maybe," Maya finally spoke, her voice resolute, "that's why they need us. Not just our knowledge, but also the stories of our mistakes. We can be a cautionary tale, a reminder of what they must avoid."

Rishi gave a curt nod, a glimmer of respect shining in his eyes. "Perhaps. But it's not just a message we need to send. We need to learn from them as well. Akashdeep has survived for millennia, untouched by our destructive impulses. They may hold the key to healing our own world."

With renewed purpose, they redoubled their efforts. Days turned into weeks as they communicated with Akashdeep, sharing their stories, their struggles, and their innovations. In return, they received knowledge on sustainable living, resource management, and forgotten technologies that could help revitalize a dying planet.

A sense of camaraderie blossomed between the two worlds. The villagers, inspired by the stories of Akashdeep's ingenuity, started implementing changes in their own lives. Solar panels scavenged from forgotten electronics were set up, rainwater harvesting systems were constructed, and vertical gardens sprouted on rooftops and walls.

One evening, as they huddled around the fire, a crackle of distorted noise erupted from the Akashvani. Rohan, his eyes glued to a complex display of flashing lights, let out a triumphant shout. "We did it!" he exclaimed. "A stable connection! We can now share visual data."

Excitedly, they activated the device's visual relay. On the screen flickered an image – a lush forest teeming with life, sunlight filtering through vibrant foliage. A gasp escaped Maya's lips. It was Akashdeep, a breathtaking panorama of a world they yearned to see firsthand.

Then, a face appeared on the screen. It was an elderly woman, her eyes filled with wisdom and a hint of sadness. She spoke in a language that flowed melodically, yet oddly familiar. The Akashvani, it seemed, was translating not just words but also emotions and intentions.

"We have received your message," she said, her voice filled with a gentle warmth. "The stories of your resilience and your spirit inspire us. We, too, have faced challenges. But together, we can learn from each other and chart a new course for both our worlds."

A tear rolled down Maya's cheek. This wasn't just a bridge between worlds; it was the first step towards a future where humanity wouldn't repeat the mistakes of the past. A future where Earth and Akashdeep could learn from each other, sharing knowledge and resources to create a sustainable existence for generations to come.

News of the successful communication spread like wildfire. Hope, once a flickering ember, began to blaze brightly in the eyes of the villagers. They were no longer just survivors clinging to a dying planet; they were pioneers, ambassadors forging a connection with a new world.

The following weeks were a whirlwind of activity. Plans were drawn up for a cultural exchange, a delegation from the village selected to visit Akashdeep. Excitement and apprehension mingled in the air. This wasn't just a journey; it was a symbol of a new beginning.

Meanwhile, Maya and Rohan, with Rishi's guidance, delved deeper into the Akashdeep technology. They learned about advanced filtration systems, clean energy generation methods, and sustainable agricultural practices. These technologies, once implemented, had the potential to transform Earth into a thriving paradise once again.

But there were challenges. The technology, though advanced, required resources that were scarce on Earth. The villagers, despite their ingenuity, lacked the infrastructure to build complex machines. A solution was needed, a bridge not just of knowledge but also of resource exchange.

One evening, as they debated under the starlit sky, Rishi spoke up, a new glint in his eyes. "There may be another way," he said, his voice filled with a newfound confidence. "The ancient texts of Akashdeep speak of a technology – a dormant portal hidden deep within the Earth."

He explained the legend, a portal that, under the right circumstances, could allow for a one-way transfer of materials. It was a risky proposition, but it offered a glimmer of hope. If they could activate the portal, it could provide the resources they needed to implement Akashdeep's technology on Earth.

The decision was momentous. A journey into the Earth's heart, a quest for a mythical portal – it felt like a story out of ancient legends. But for Maya, Rohan, and the villagers, it wasn't a story; it was their reality. They were no longer just scavengers and dreamers; they were the architects of a new future, a bridge between worlds.

With renewed determination, they embarked on this new challenge, their hearts filled with the hope of a brighter tomorrow, a future where the skies of Earth could once again shimmer as brightly as the golden sun of Akashdeep. The journey would be fraught with danger, but the stakes had never been higher. The fate of two worlds rested on their shoulders.

The quest for the dormant portal plunged Maya, Rohan, and Rishi deep into the heart of the Himalayas. Guided by ancient texts deciphered by Rishi and translated by the Akashvani, they ventured into treacherous caverns, navigating through labyrinthine tunnels and clinging to precarious ledges. The air grew thick and stale, the only light provided by flickering headlamps that cast grotesque shadows on the damp cave walls.

Fear gnawed at their edges. The villagers, used to the harshness of the mountains, were unnerved by the suffocating darkness and the unseen creatures that skittered beyond the reach of their light. Maya, ever resourceful, kept their spirits high by sharing stories of Akashdeep, tales of shimmering waterfalls and vibrant flora that fueled their hope.

Days bled into nights, the passage of time marked by the rhythmic drip of water and the creak of their boots on uneven ground. One evening, exhaustion etched on their faces, they stumbled into a vast cavern unlike any they had seen before. Sunlight, filtered through a crack in the ceiling high above, illuminated an awe-inspiring sight.

Crystal formations, shimmering with an otherworldly glow, adorned the cavern walls. In the center, a structure of smooth, black metal pulsated with a faint energy, mirroring the technology of Akashdeep. This was it. The dormant portal.

Excitement warred with trepidation. The texts spoke of activating the portal with a specific sequence of symbols, a code etched on the metal surface. Rishi, his face alight with a newfound purpose, stepped forward. Years spent studying ancient texts finally had a tangible application.

He meticulously traced the symbols with his finger, muttering a string of cryptic words retrieved from the Akashvani translations. The cavern walls vibrated with a low hum as the symbols glowed with an eerie green light. A crackle of energy filled the air, and the metal structure began to rise, revealing a swirling vortex of iridescent light.

A gasp escaped Maya's lips. The portal was activated. But with activation came a surge of uncertainty. The texts were clear – the portal allowed for a one-way transfer of materials. They could send resources up, but there was no guarantee of a return path.

A heavy silence descended upon the group. They had come so far, but the final step involved a monumental leap of faith. Looking around at the weary faces, Maya knew they needed a leader.

"We have a choice," she declared, her voice echoing in the vast cavern. "We can turn back, keep the knowledge of the portal hidden. But what does that achieve? Akashdeep has shared their knowledge freely. Shouldn't we do the same?"

"We can learn a lot from their technology," Rohan added, his voice filled with a youthful optimism. "It could be the key to healing Earth, to giving future generations a chance."

Rishi remained silent, his gaze fixed on the swirling portal. Finally, he spoke, his voice laced with a quiet determination. "I failed once," he said, his words carrying the weight of his past. "I couldn't save my world. But maybe, just maybe, by opening this portal, we can save both."

His words resonated with the group. They had come too far to turn back now. With a collective nod, they decided to proceed. They gathered the resources they had brought – scavenged metals, purified water, and carefully preserved plant seeds.

One by one, they fed the materials into the portal, a silent exchange between worlds. With each offering, the energy in the cavern intensified. As the last item disappeared into the swirling vortex, the portal pulsed with an blinding light before collapsing inward, leaving behind a faint hum in its wake.

They had done it. They had made the leap of faith. But now, the question loomed – would it be enough? Would Akashdeep receive their message of trust and collaboration? Only time would tell.

Dejected but hopeful, they began the arduous journey back to the village. The silence that had filled the cavern now resonated within them. They had taken a step towards a brighter future, but the path ahead remained shrouded in uncertainty.

As they emerged from the darkness of the caves, blinking in the sunlight, a cheer erupted from the village below. A delegation from Akashdeep, cloaked in their shimmering white robes, stood before the villagers, a symbol of the connection they had forged.

Tears welled up in Maya's eyes. Their journey, fraught with danger and uncertainty, had borne fruit. The bridge between worlds wasn't just a technological marvel; it was a testament to the power of hope, trust, and the indomitable human spirit.

The future was uncertain, but one thing was clear – the future was no longer a solitary struggle for survival. It was a shared journey, a collaboration between two worlds, each holding the key to the other's redemption.

The arrival of the Akashdeep delegation marked the beginning of a new era. Knowledge and resources flowed freely. With the help of Akashdeep's advanced technology, the villagers began implementing sustainable practices. Solar panels gleamed on rooftops, vertical gardens sprouted on previously barren walls, and rainwater harvesting systems ensured a steady supply of clean water.

The transformation of the village became a beacon of hope, attracting others from nearby settlements. Slowly, a network of sustainable communities began to take shape, spreading across the once-polluted landscape.

Meanwhile, Maya, Rohan, and Rishi worked closely with the Akashdeep delegation. They learned about advanced filtration systems that could cleanse the polluted air, efficient energy generation methods that harnessed the power of the sun and wind, and innovative agricultural techniques that yielded bountiful harvests with minimal environmental impact.

Implementing these technologies on a larger scale proved challenging. The infrastructure was lacking, and the knowledge gap between the two worlds was vast. But with unwavering determination, they developed a training program, teaching the villagers the intricacies of Akashdeep technology and fostering a generation of eco-warriors.

As years passed, the once-bleak landscape began to show signs of healing. The air grew cleaner, the skies less choked with smog. Trees, painstakingly nurtured by the villagers, sprouted green tendrils against the grey backdrop, offering a glimpse of a future where nature and humanity could co-exist in harmony.

News of the transformation spread like wildfire, reaching the ears of the city dwellers trapped in their smog-filled metropolises. Inspired by the success of the village, pockets of resistance began to emerge. People demanded a change, a shift towards clean energy and sustainable living.

The journey, however, wasn't without its challenges. Powerful corporations, their profits threatened by the shift towards clean energy, sought to maintain the status quo. Political leaders, swayed by the powerful lobbyists, were slow to embrace change.

But the movement for a greener future had gained momentum. The villagers, once mere survivors, became symbols of hope. Maya, Rohan, and Rishi, once explorers and scavengers, became the voice of a generation yearning for a cleaner world.

The fight for a sustainable future was far from over. But as Maya stood on a rooftop overlooking the village, now a thriving hub of green technology, she felt a flicker of pride. The bridge they built, a bridge not just of technology but of collaboration and shared dreams, had sparked a movement. A movement that, brick by brick, breath by breath, was beginning to heal a broken planet.

Chapter 4: Echoes of Unity

Decades had passed since the pivotal events in the Himalayan village. What began as a desperate plea for help had blossomed into a global movement. Earth, once choked by pollution and despair, was slowly taking tentative steps towards healing.

Maya, now a seasoned leader with streaks of silver in her once vibrant hair, stood before a gathering of delegates from across the globe. Gone were the days of scavenging for scraps in the shadow of towering smokestacks. Now, she addressed a room filled with representatives from countries once divided by greed and national interests, now united by a common goal – the preservation of their planet.

"The journey has been long and arduous," Maya began, her voice resonating with quiet authority. "But the fruits of our collaboration are beginning to blossom. The polluted skies of yesterday are giving way to a clearer future."

She gestured towards a holographic map projected in the center of the room. It depicted Earth, no longer a uniform grey, but a tapestry of green patches interspersed with pockets of blue and gold – thriving eco-communities, vast solar farms, and wind energy installations.

The key to this transformation lay in the knowledge exchange facilitated by the bridge. Akashdeep's advanced technology, adapted for Earth's needs, had revolutionized every aspect of life. Clean air filtration systems hummed in megalopolises, once barren deserts buzzed with life thanks to efficient water harvesting techniques, and vertical farms produced enough food to feed a growing population.

But the road to a sustainable future wasn't paved solely with technology. It was built on a foundation of collaboration and a collective shift in consciousness. The message from Akashdeep, a cautionary tale of a society's self-destruction, had resonated deeply. Educational programs emphasizing environmental responsibility had become a cornerstone of every nation's curriculum.

However, the fight was far from over. Powerful corporations, their profits threatened by the shift towards clean energy, continued to lobby relentlessly. Pockets of resistance, fueled by misinformation and a fear of change, still existed.

"Our success has also brought unforeseen challenges," Maya continued, her voice turning stern. "There are those who seek to exploit this new technology for personal gain, ignoring the spirit of collaboration that brought us this far."

A murmur of agreement rippled through the room. A delegate from a developing nation rose, his voice filled with concern. "The technology, while a blessing, remains inaccessible to many. What good is clean air if it only graces the skies of the wealthy nations?"

Maya nodded, acknowledging the validity of his concern. The bridge between Earth and Akashdeep had facilitated knowledge transfer, but equitable access remained a hurdle.

"The responsibility lies with all of us here," Maya declared. "We must work together to ensure that this technology serves humanity, not just a privileged few. Knowledge sharing and resource allocation must be at the heart of our collaboration."

She proposed a new initiative – a global fund, fueled by contributions from all nations, to ensure that the benefits of clean technology reached every corner of the globe. The proposal was met with enthusiastic applause.

The meeting room buzzed with renewed energy. Delegates huddled, discussing implementation strategies, sharing best practices, and forging new alliances. Maya, a symbol of hope who had witnessed the very worst of human greed, now looked upon a room filled with the seeds of a brighter future being sown.

However, amidst the optimism, a shadow of unease lingered in Maya's heart. A piece of the puzzle remained incomplete. The portal deep within the Himalayas had fulfilled its purpose, sending resources to Akashdeep. But there had been no response, no word about the fate of their message, no sign of reciprocation.

As the delegates dispersed, Maya found herself drawn to Rohan, his hair now streaked with grey but his youthful spirit undimmed. He, too, seemed preoccupied.

"Do you think they received it?" Rohan asked, his voice tinged with uncertainty. "Our message, our plea for collaboration?"

Maya shook her head, a knot of worry tightening in her stomach. "We don't know. Maybe they're facing challenges of their own."

A heavy silence descended upon them. The success they celebrated was built upon a one-way communication. The bridge they had built seemed to have a missing link.

"We can't let that stop us," Maya finally said, her voice resolute. "We've come too far to give in to doubt. We'll continue building a sustainable future here, on Earth. Maybe one day, Akashdeep will be ready to join us."

Rohan nodded, his eyes filled with a renewed determination. "We built a bridge, Maya. Maybe it's time to build another one. One that doesn't rely on technology, but on a shared yearning for peace and a sustainable future."

Rohan's suggestion ignited a new fire within Maya. A bridge built not of technology, but of understanding, a cultural exchange that transcended the physical limitations. The idea was audacious, yet it resonated with a deep longing within her – the desire to truly connect with the people of Akashdeep, to understand their story, their struggles, and their triumphs.

The concept gained traction amongst the delegates. Many, inspired by the success of the Earth-Akashdeep collaboration, saw the value in fostering a deeper connection. A committee was formed, tasked with developing a plan for a cultural exchange program.

The challenge was daunting. Communication, so far, had been limited to the exchange of technical data and messages. Understanding the nuances of Akashdeep culture, their art, music, and social structures, would require a different approach.

Days turned into weeks as the committee brainstormed. Finally, a solution emerged – an artistic exchange. Earth would send a group of artists – musicians, painters, and storytellers – to Akashdeep, carrying with them the essence of human creativity on their home planet. In return, Akashdeep would send their own artistic delegation.

The selection process was rigorous. Artists were chosen not just for their talent, but also for their ability to bridge cultural divides, to express the human experience in a way that transcended language barriers. Among those chosen was Maya herself. Her journey from scavenger to leader, her embodiment of the human spirit's resilience, made her a powerful symbol for the Earth delegation.

The day of departure arrived, a mix of excitement and apprehension hanging in the air. Standing at the foot of the newly constructed launch facility, a marvel of sustainable technology, Maya looked up at the sleek spacecraft gleaming in the sunlight. This wasn't just a journey to another world; it was a leap of faith, a bridge built on music, stories, and the universal language of human emotion.

The journey through the cosmos was a blur of starlight and swirling nebulae. Days turned into weeks as they traversed the vast emptiness of space, fueled by a shared purpose and a yearning for connection.

Finally, a breathtaking sight filled the viewport – Akashdeep, a jewel suspended in the inky blackness, its vibrant bioluminescent glow a stark contrast to the barren landscape of Earth. As the spacecraft descended, a wave of awe washed over Maya. This was the world they had yearned to see, a testament to humanity's potential for innovation and sustainability.

They were greeted with a warmth that surprised them. The Akashdeep delegation, cloaked not in their usual white robes but in garments adorned with vibrant colors and intricate patterns, welcomed them with music and gestures of friendship.

The following days were a whirlwind of cultural exchange. Earth's artists showcased their talents – Maya, with a voice seasoned by experience, narrated stories of Earth's past, its struggles, and its triumphs. The music of Earth, a blend of traditional instruments and modern electronic beats, filled the air. In return, the people of Akashdeep shared their own art forms – ethereal music played on instruments that seemed to resonate with the very fabric of space, and stories woven with light and movement, depicting a history far richer than anything Maya could have imagined.

As days turned into weeks, a deep understanding began to blossom. They discovered shared values – a love for nature, a yearning for peace, and a deep respect for creativity. They learned of Akashdeep's own struggles – a constant battle against a dwindling energy source, a legacy of the war that had ravaged their home planet long ago.

The exchange program wasn't just about artistic expression; it was about empathy. They saw themselves reflected in each other's stories, their vulnerabilities and triumphs laid bare. The bridge they built wasn't just a physical structure; it was a bridge of hearts and minds.

On the day of their departure, a bittersweet feeling hung in the air. They were leaving behind newfound friends and a world that, despite its challenges, held a unique beauty. But they were also returning home, carrying with them not just memories, but a renewed sense of purpose.

Back on Earth, the artists' experiences sparked a global phenomenon. Artworks inspired by Akashdeep's beauty and stories of their struggles adorned buildings and public spaces. Music that echoed the universal language of emotions resonated across cultures. The cultural exchange program had achieved what technology alone could not – it had fostered a sense of unity, a shared purpose that transcended national borders.

Years passed, and the collaboration between Earth and Akashdeep continued to flourish. The artistic exchange program expanded, fostering a deeper understanding between the two worlds. Technology continued to evolve, with both planets sharing advancements for the betterment of all.

One evening, as Maya gazed upon the star-dusted night sky, a familiar crackle erupted from the communication console. Her heart leaped – a message from Akashdeep! But this time, it wasn't a stream of data or a projected image. Instead, a melody filled the room, a hauntingly beautiful song unlike anything she'd heard before.

As the music washed over her, images flickered across the screen – swirling colors, intricate patterns, and landscapes bathed in an ethereal glow. It wasn't a literal translation, but an emotional one, a response to the stories and music Earth had sent years ago.

A tear welled up in Maya's eye. The bridge they built, the bridge of hearts and minds, had finally reached its destination. Akashdeep wasn't just silent observers; they were actively participating in the dialogue.

The following days were a flurry of activity. Scientists deciphered the complex musical code, translating the emotions embedded within the melody. It spoke of gratitude for the shared knowledge, of a deep respect for Earth's resilience, and a yearning for a future where the two worlds could collaborate not just out of necessity, but out of a shared love for life and creativity.

The message ignited a renewed sense of purpose on Earth. Artists responded in kind, composing music that resonated with themes of unity and hope. Scientists delved deeper into communication technologies, seeking ways to bridge the physical gap between the worlds.

Years passed, and the collaboration continued to evolve. Joint artistic projects emerged, a symphony of Earthly instruments and Akashdeep's ethereal soundscapes echoing across both planets. Scientific advancements allowed for real-time communication, fostering a sense of closeness that transcended the vastness of space.

One momentous day, a new message arrived from Akashdeep – not a melody, but a holographic projection. An Akashdeep delegate, her face etched with wisdom and kindness, addressed the people of Earth.

"For generations," she began, her voice resonating with warmth, "we have walked separate paths, burdened by the weight of our past. But through art, music, and the stories we shared, we have built a bridge not just of technology, but of understanding. Today, we stand on the threshold of a new era, an era of collaboration, of shared prosperity, and of a united future for all who call these stars their home."

A wave of elation rippled across Earth. The dream Maya had nurtured for decades, the dream of a united future for humanity across the stars, was finally within reach. The bridge they built, a bridge forged not just of metal and technology, but of empathy and shared dreams, had become a beacon of hope, a testament to the power of human connection in the vast expanse of the universe.

The future remained uncertain, but one thing was clear – humanity, once a species teetering on the brink of self-destruction, had found a new path. A path illuminated not just by the light of the stars, but by the unwavering flame of unity and a shared yearning for a future where humanity could, once again, exist in harmony with itself and the universe around it.

The message from Akashdeep, a response not just in words but in emotions, sent a wave of elation across Earth. The bridge they had built, a bridge of hearts and minds, had resonated across the vast expanse of space. But the question remained - how would they translate this emotional connection into a tangible reality?

The answer came from an unexpected source – a young artist named Kai. Inspired by the Akashdeep message, he created a series of paintings that captured the essence of the human experience – the vibrant energy of bustling cities, the quiet serenity of nature, and the unyielding human spirit in the face of adversity.

His artwork, titled "Echoes of Unity," resonated with people across the globe. They saw themselves reflected in his brushstrokes, their hopes and dreams intertwined with the message of collaboration. The paintings became a rallying cry, a call to action to further solidify the bond between Earth and Akashdeep.

Fueled by this renewed sense of purpose, scientists from both worlds delved deeper into communication technologies. Their shared goal was to create a real-time connection, a way to bridge the physical gap and foster a sense of immediate closeness.

Years of research culminated in the unveiling of the Akashnet – a complex network of satellites and relays that stretched across the vast interstellar space. It wasn't just a technological marvel; it was a digital tapestry woven with the threads of hope and collaboration.

The Akashnet revolutionized communication. Live conferences were held, fostering discussions and debates on scientific advancements, artistic collaborations bloomed in real-time, and cultural exchanges transcended the limitations of pre-recorded messages.

But the Akashnet's true potential was realized when a disaster struck Akashdeep. An unforeseen solar flare triggered a cascade of malfunctions in their energy grid, plunging entire cities into darkness. Panic threatened to engulf the population.

However, the Akashnet proved its worth. Earth scientists, alerted in real-time, were able to offer assistance. Through video calls and data exchange, they helped Akashdeep engineers troubleshoot the problem and implement emergency protocols.

The crisis, a stark reminder of their shared vulnerability, further solidified the bond between the two worlds. Earth and Akashdeep weren't just collaborators; they were lifelines, safety nets for each other in the face of unforeseen threats.

The experience sparked a new initiative – the Interstellar Emergency Response Team (IERT). Composed of Earth and Akashdeep personnel, the IERT was trained to respond to disasters and emergencies, a testament to their commitment to mutual support.

Years passed, marked by a continuous exchange of knowledge, technology, and art. The once-distant world of Akashdeep became a familiar presence in Earth's daily life. Their art, their music, and their stories became an integral part of Earth's culture, a constant reminder of the bridge they had built.

One day, a new message arrived from Akashdeep, not through the Akashnet, but through a newly developed technology – a prototype for interstellar travel. It wasn't a perfected system, but it held the promise of a physical connection, a two-way journey that transcended the limitations of digital communication.

A wave of excitement swept across Earth. The dream Maya and her generation had nurtured for decades - the dream of walking hand-in-hand with the people of Akashdeep - was finally within reach. The bridge they built, a bridge of hearts, minds, and now technology, had paved the way for a future where humanity wouldn't just gaze upon the stars, but explore them together.

This was just the beginning. The journey ahead would be fraught with challenges, but one thing was certain – humanity, once a species divided by greed and conflict, had found a new path. A path illuminated by the light of the stars, and the unwavering flame of unity that burned brighter with every step they took towards a shared future.

The prototype vessel, christened "Echoes of Unity" in honor of Kai's paintings, looked like a sleek silver arrow poised to pierce the veil of space. It was a marvel of combined technology – Earth's sustainable energy systems merged with Akashdeep's advanced propulsion technology, a testament to their unwavering collaboration.

Choosing the crew for the inaugural voyage became a global spectacle. Scientists, engineers, artists, and diplomats were nominated, each representing a facet of the newfound unity between Earth and Akashdeep. From Earth, Maya, a symbol of resilience and hope, was chosen as the mission commander. A young scientist named Amara, whose work on sustainable energy had captivated both worlds, was selected as the lead engineer. And alongside them was Kai, the artist whose "Echoes of Unity" series had ignited a global desire for connection.

From Akashdeep, a seasoned captain named Lyra, known for her calm demeanor and strategic brilliance, would co-pilot the vessel. Joining her was a renowned astrophysicist named Elara, whose research on interstellar travel had laid the groundwork for this historic voyage. And finally, a young musician named Kiran, whose music resonated with themes of unity and exploration, was chosen to represent Akashdeep's artistic spirit.

The launch day arrived, a day etched in history as humanity embarked on its first interstellar voyage. Millions gathered to witness the momentous event, their eyes glued to screens as the Echoes of Unity roared to life, a testament to the collective human spirit.

The journey was a blur of starlight and cosmic wonders. The crew, a diverse group from two planets, bonded over shared meals, exchanged stories of their home worlds, and marveled at the breathtaking sights unfolding before them.

They were not just explorers; they were ambassadors, carrying the hopes and dreams of their respective worlds.

Days turned into weeks, and a sense of camaraderie blossomed among the crew. Maya and Lyra, veterans in their own right, co-led the team with a sense of shared purpose. Amara and Elara, their minds brimming with scientific curiosity, worked closely to monitor the ship's systems and analyze the vast swathes of data gathered during the journey. Kai and Kiran, their artistic souls yearning for expression, collaborated on a musical piece inspired by their cosmic voyage.

Finally, after months of travel, a familiar glow filled the viewscreen – Akashdeep, no longer a distant image in the cosmos, but a vibrant world waiting to be explored. A collective cheer erupted in the control room, a mixture of relief and excitement washing over the crew. They had made it.

The landing on Akashdeep was a joyous occasion. The people of Akashdeep, their faces filled with a mix of wonder and familiarity, welcomed the Earth delegation with open arms. For the first time, humans from two different worlds stood side-by-side, not just on a digital screen, but on solid ground, a symbol of the unity they had so painstakingly built.

The following days were a whirlwind of cultural exchange on a grand scale. Earthlings marveled at the technological advancements that co-existed with the natural beauty of Akashdeep, while Akashdeepers were mesmerized by the vibrant energy and artistic expressions of Earth.

However, amidst the celebrations, a shadow lingered. Akashdeep, while technologically advanced, was facing a new challenge – their energy source, rejuvenated by the Dyson Sphere, was depleting at a faster rate than anticipated. The clock was ticking, and the future of both worlds remained uncertain.

This shared struggle solidified their bond even further. Scientists from both worlds, fueled by a renewed sense of urgency, pooled their knowledge and resources. Maya, reflecting on the journey that led them here, proposed a radical idea – a daring mission to explore a nearby nebula, rumored to harbor a dormant black hole, a potential source of immense energy.

This mission, fraught with risks and unknowns, would require an unprecedented level of collaboration. But with their backs against the wall, the crew of the Echoes of Unity, ambassadors of two worlds bound by a shared destiny, volunteered to lead the expedition.

As the Echoes of Unity, once a symbol of unity, readied itself for this pivotal mission, a hush fell over the gathered crowd. This wasn't just a scientific expedition; it was a voyage into the unknown, a quest for a future not just for Earth and Akashdeep, but for humanity's continued existence. The bridge they built, a bridge forged not just of technology and art, but of shared dreams and the unwavering human spirit, now faced its ultimate test.

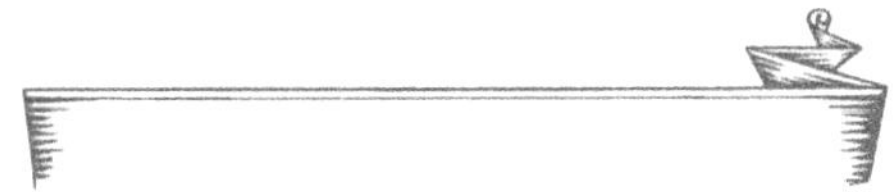

Chapter 5: Whispers Across Worlds

The decision to venture into the swirling nebula, a cosmic graveyard where stars went to die, sent a wave of apprehension through the crew of the Echoes of Unity. The potential rewards – a source of near-infinite energy to sustain both Earth and Akashdeep – were undeniable. But the risks were equally daunting. The nebula, a chaotic dance of charged particles and stellar remnants, held dangers unknown, its secrets jealously guarded by the swirling gas and dust.

As Maya, the seasoned commander, addressed the crew in the ship's briefing room, her voice held a steady resolve. "This mission," she began, her gaze sweeping across the diverse group, "is unlike any we've undertaken before. We venture into the unknown, guided by scientific theories and a flicker of hope. The fate of our worlds rests on our shoulders."

Lyra, the Akashdeep co-pilot, her dark eyes filled with quiet determination, nodded in agreement. "We will face challenges," she added, her voice laced with a hint of Akashdeep's melodic cadence, "but together, as a united crew, we will overcome them."

The weeks leading up to the mission were a flurry of activity. Amara and Elara, the lead scientists, meticulously planned their research protocols, eager to unravel the mysteries of the nebula. Kai and Kiran, their artistic spirits yearning to capture the essence of this celestial spectacle, prepared their tools, determined to translate the nebula's untamed beauty into art.

The day of departure arrived, shrouded in an air of nervous anticipation. The crew, clad in their specially designed suits, gathered for a final send-off. From Earth, millions watched the live feed, their hearts pounding in unison with the crew. From Akashdeep, families and friends gathered, their silent prayers echoing across the vast expanse of space.

As the Echoes of Unity entered the nebula, the once vibrant viewscreen was replaced by a swirling tapestry of color. Glowing tendrils of gas, their hues defying earthly definition, danced wildly before them. The ship lurched and tilted as it navigated the unpredictable currents of charged particles, a symphony of warnings and alerts filling the control room.

Amara, her brow furrowed in concentration, monitored the energy readings. "There's something... different here," she announced, her voice laced with excitement. "The readings... they're off the charts."

Elara, her eyes glued to the holographic map projected before her, confirmed her suspicions. "There's a massive energy signature at the heart of the nebula, far exceeding what we anticipated."

A wave of elation rippled through the crew. Could this be the dormant black hole they were searching for? The answer lay ahead, shrouded in the swirling chaos of the nebula.

Maya, her gaze fixed on the swirling vortex before them, felt a surge of hope. The journey had been fraught with challenges, but they were on the verge of a breakthrough. The bridge they built, a bridge of collaboration forged across the vast expanse of space, had led them here, to the precipice of a discovery that could ensure the future of their worlds.

But as they ventured deeper into the nebula, the once mesmerizing spectacle began to feel oppressive. The swirling gas seemed to pulsate with an unsettling energy, a low hum resonating through the ship, sending shivers down their spines. The bridge, a beacon of hope for so long, now felt like a precarious tightrope stretched across a chaotic abyss.

The deeper they ventured into the nebula, the more the fabric of reality seemed to unravel. The vibrant, swirling gas that had initially captivated them now took on a menacing tinge. Strange formations flickered in and out of existence, phantom images shimmering on the periphery of their vision. The low hum that had filled the ship escalated into a disconcerting drone, a constant reminder of the unknown forces they were brushing against.

An unsettling tension gripped the crew. Even the calm and collected Maya couldn't ignore the prickling sensation of unease crawling up her spine. The nebula, once a potential source of salvation, now felt like a malevolent entity, testing their resolve.

Technical glitches began to plague the ship. Gauges flickered erratically, instruments malfunctioned, and the communication systems sputtered, cutting them off from the outside world. They were isolated, adrift in a sea of swirling energy, their only lifeline a vessel that seemed to be succumbing to the nebula's malevolent influence.

In the face of these challenges, the crew's unity, forged through months of collaboration, became their anchor. Amara and Elara, their scientific training holding firm, worked tirelessly to diagnose the source of the malfunctions, their voices a reassuring hum amidst the chaos. Kai and

Kiran, their artistic talents transcending the technical limitations, created projections that served as makeshift communication channels, their drawings conveying the urgency of their situation.

Maya and Lyra, their leadership tested but not broken, rallied the crew. Their calm voices cut through the rising panic, reminding everyone of their mission's importance. "We came here together," Maya declared, her voice echoing through the control room, "and we will face this together. Our worlds, our future, depend on it."

Inspired by Maya's words, the crew redoubled their efforts. They rerouted power, bypassed malfunctioning systems, and relied on their combined ingenuity to keep the Echoes of Unity afloat. Slowly, painstakingly, they regained a semblance of control.

But as they neared the source of the energy signature, a new set of challenges emerged. The swirling gas became denser, visibility dropped drastically, and the low hum morphed into a deafening roar, threatening to overwhelm their senses. Navigating became a matter of instinct, relying on readings from their salvaged instruments and the faint glow emanating from the object at the nebula's heart.

Finally, they emerged from the swirling gas cloud, and a sight of awe-inspiring terror greeted them. Before them, a colossal black hole, its event horizon a swirling vortex of darkness, pulsed with an energy far exceeding their wildest dreams. But surrounding the black hole, like moths drawn to a flame, were dozens of derelict ships, their hulls bearing a striking resemblance to the Akashdeep vessels depicted in ancient texts.

A wave of realization washed over Maya and Lyra. This wasn't a haven of potential energy; it was a graveyard. The Akashdeep of old, lured by the promise of limitless power, had met their demise at the edge of this singularity. The whispers across worlds, the stories passed down through generations, suddenly held a chilling truth.

The bridge they built, a bridge of collaboration, now stretched across a vast chasm of time and consequence. The history of Akashdeep, a cautionary tale etched in the wreckage of lost vessels, hung heavy in the air. They had come seeking a solution, but had instead stumbled upon a chilling reminder of the potential dangers that lay hidden in the vast expanse of space.

The discovery of the Akashdeep graveyard cast a heavy pall over the crew of the Echoes of Unity. The awe of witnessing a colossal black hole was overshadowed by the chilling truth it revealed – the tragic fate of a civilization lured by the promise of limitless energy. The bridge they built, a bridge of collaboration, now seemed to span a dark chasm of time and consequence.

A heavy silence descended upon the control room. Even the ever-optimistic Kai and Kiran struggled to find inspiration in the face of such a bleak revelation. The echoes of the past, the whispers across worlds spoken through the wreckage of ancient ships, resonated with a profound sense of loss.

But amidst the despair, a flicker of determination ignited in Maya's eyes. They had come too far, risked too much, to simply turn back. She addressed the crew, her voice unwavering. "This isn't the end," she declared, "it's a turning point. We can learn from the mistakes of the past, forge a new path for our future."

Lyra, her resolve mirroring Maya's, nodded in agreement. "We came here seeking a solution," she added, "and perhaps the solution isn't just about harnessing immense energy, but about utilizing it with wisdom and responsibility."

Amara and Elara, their scientific minds churning, began to re-evaluate their data. The wreckage of the Akashdeep vessels, though silent testaments to a tragic past, held valuable clues. Perhaps, they theorized, by studying the remnants of their technology, they could glean insights into the dangers of unbridled power and develop safer ways to tap into the nebula's energy reserves.

Kai and Kiran, their artistic spirits responding to the newfound purpose, began crafting a series of holographic projections. These weren't just images of the black hole and the derelict ships; they were a visual narrative, a cautionary tale woven with elements of beauty and destruction. They hoped this message, transcending language barriers, would serve as a reminder to both Earth and Akashdeep of the importance of using power responsibly.

Days turned into weeks as the crew meticulously analyzed their findings. They weren't just scientists and artists on an exploratory mission; they were ambassadors, carrying the weight of two civilizations on their shoulders.

Finally, they emerged from the nebula, forever changed by their experience. The swirling gas, once a source of fear, now held a bittersweet beauty. They carried with them not just data and images, but a newfound wisdom – a responsibility to ensure their bridge of collaboration wasn't just a path to a shared future, but a pathway towards a future built on sustainable energy practices and a deep respect for the vast and often unforgiving forces of the universe.

As the Echoes of Unity emerged from the nebula and re-established communication with Earth and Akashdeep, a wave of relief washed over both worlds. Their heroes had returned, not with a solution they initially envisioned, but with a lesson far more valuable. The whispers across worlds, once a cautionary tale shrouded in mystery, now became a shared narrative, a stark reminder of the consequences of unchecked ambition.

The mission to the nebula marked a turning point. The focus shifted from harvesting the black hole's energy to developing alternative, sustainable sources. Scientists from Earth and Akashdeep, fueled by a renewed sense of purpose, collaborated on projects harnessing solar energy, geothermal power, and even the untapped potential of fusion technology. The bridge they built, once envisioned as a path to a shared energy source, transformed into a platform for cooperative scientific advancement, a testament to their commitment to a sustainable future.

Years passed, marked by advancements in clean energy technology and a deep-seated respect for the delicate balance of the universe. The echoes of the past, the whispers across worlds, continued to resonate, serving as a constant reminder of the Akashdeep graveyard and the cautionary tale it held. The bridge they built, a bridge forged not just of technology and art, but of shared experiences and a newfound wisdom, ensured their future remained bright, a testament to the enduring power of collaboration in the face of the unknown.

The crew of the Echoes of Unity returned to Earth as heroes, not just for their daring mission but for the profound wisdom they brought back. Their story, a saga of courage, collaboration, and a hard-learned lesson, resonated across the globe. Schools incorporated the Echoes of Unity's experience into their curriculum, teaching children the importance of responsible energy use and the dangers of unchecked ambition. Governments re-evaluated their energy policies, prioritizing sustainability and shifting focus towards renewable resources.

Akashdeep underwent a similar transformation. The whispers across worlds, the chilling tale of their ancestors' demise, became a rallying cry for change. Their focus shifted from exploiting resources to nurturing them, developing technologies that harnessed the power of their sun more efficiently while minimizing environmental impact.

The Echoes of Unity itself became a symbol of this new era. The ship, once a vessel for exploration, was transformed into a mobile research platform. It traveled between Earth and Akashdeep, facilitating the exchange of knowledge and scientific advancements. Onboard laboratories bustled with activity as scientists from both worlds collaborated on projects to develop clean energy solutions.

Years turned into decades, and the bridge they built continued to evolve. Joint artistic projects flourished, a symphony of Earthly instruments and Akashdeep's ethereal soundscapes echoing across both planets. Educational programs fostered cultural exchange, creating a generation of young people who viewed Earth and Akashdeep not as separate entities, but as two halves of a whole.

One momentous day, a new project was announced - Project Odyssey. A joint venture between Earth and Akashdeep, it aimed to build a self-sustaining space station, a neutral ground for humanity's burgeoning interplanetary society. The Echoes of Unity, a veteran of countless journeys, was chosen as the cornerstone of this ambitious project.

As the construction of Project Odyssey began, a sense of hope and optimism filled the air. This wasn't just a space station; it was a symbol of a future where humanity, once a species divided by conflict and greed, had learned from its mistakes. The bridge they built, a bridge forged not just of technology and art, but of shared experience and a deep respect for the vastness of space, had become a permanent structure, a testament to the enduring human spirit.

Gazing upon the partially constructed Project Odyssey from the observation deck of the Echoes of Unity, Maya, her face etched with the passage of time but her eyes still sparkling with a youthful fire, reflected on their journey. They had faced challenges, stumbled upon unexpected dangers, and ultimately emerged stronger, more united. The whispers across worlds, once a whisper of conflict, had now morphed into a chorus of collaboration, a testament to the potential of humanity when it set its sights on a common goal.

The future remained uncertain, filled with the promise of new discoveries and the constant allure of the unknown. But one thing was certain - humanity, once a species teetering on the brink of self-destruction, had found a new path. A path illuminated not just by the light of distant stars, but by the unwavering flame of unity and a shared responsibility for the future of humanity and the universe it inhabited. The bridge they built, a bridge that transcended distance and time, served as a beacon of hope, a testament to the potential for collaboration and the enduring human spirit that yearned to explore, to learn, and to reach for the stars, not in conquest, but in harmony.

About the Author

Mrigendra Bharti, born on June 29, 2004, in South Delhi, India, is a multifaceted individual recognized as the owner of Mrigendra Bharti Group InfoTech India Co. Pvt Ltd. Beyond his entrepreneurial endeavors, he is a distinguished music producer, director, and a budding writer.

Embarking on his professional journey at a young age, Mrigendra Bharti's visionary leadership has led to the establishment of several successful ventures, including Croma Music Series Entertainment, Sellbrochure, Fauget Innovative, and more.

What sets Mrigendra apart is his early initiation into the world of business. His foray into the unknown realms of entrepreneurship began during his 10th-grade years, where he delved into the music industry. This initial venture laid the foundation for subsequent achievements, showcasing his dedication and resilience.

Having honed his skills in music, Mrigendra Bharti not only demonstrated significant growth in his craft but also expanded his professional network. His passion extends beyond music, encompassing app and website development, as well as graphic design.

Fueled by his creative aspirations, Mrigendra established the Mrigendra Bharti Group, a company specializing in website and app development. Currently, he collaborates with a dedicated team, collectively working on ambitious projects that promise innovation and excellence.

Mrigendra's journey serves as an inspiration, particularly for today's students, highlighting the potential of youthful determination and the ability to transform innovative ideas into successful businesses. As he continues to make strides in various domains, Mrigendra Bharti remains a dynamic force, contributing vibrancy to the realms of business, music, and technology.

Read more at https://www.imwriter-mrigendra.rf.gd.

www.ingramcontent.com/pod-product-compliance
Lightning Source LLC
Chambersburg PA
CBHW052209150726
48002CB00003B/1142